Once, in **A BOOK** by **MORDICAI GERSTEIN**, published by Roaring Brook Press, New York, there lived a family of characters.

There was a father and a mother,
a girl and a boy,
and some pets.

When the book was closed
it was night in the book,
and the family slept.

When the book was open
it was morning, and
the family woke up.

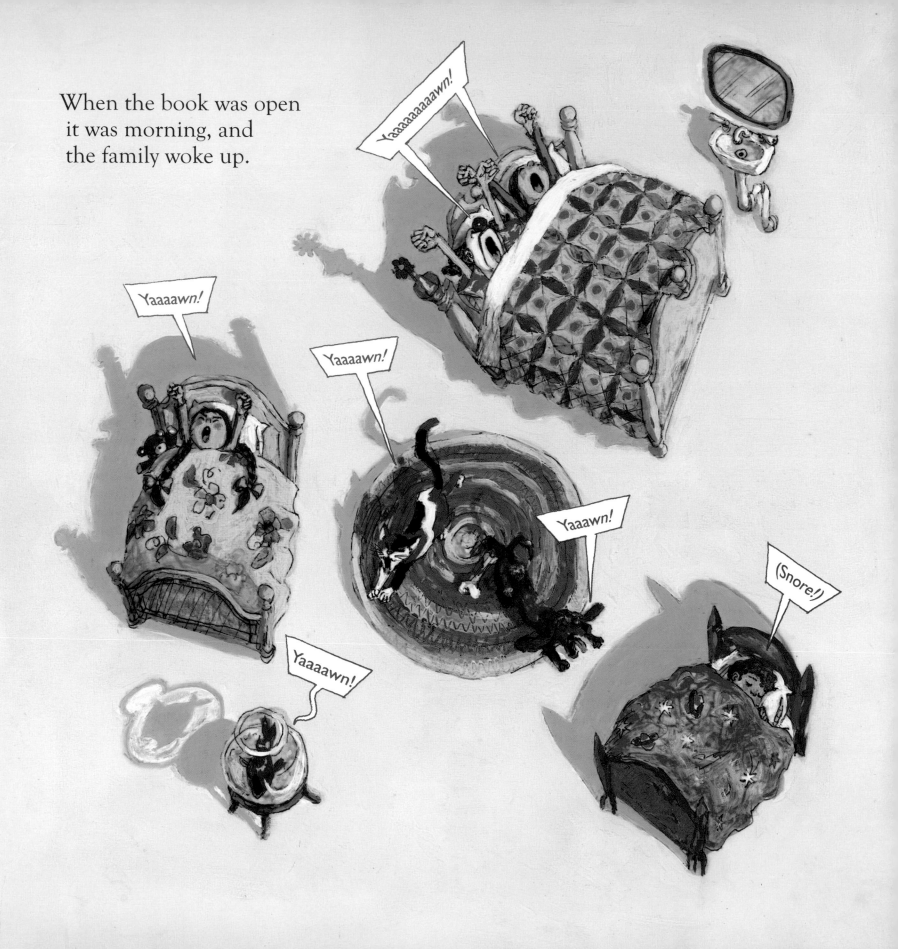

They did all the things families do when they get up and begin the day.

One morning the girl
asked about something
that had been troubling her.

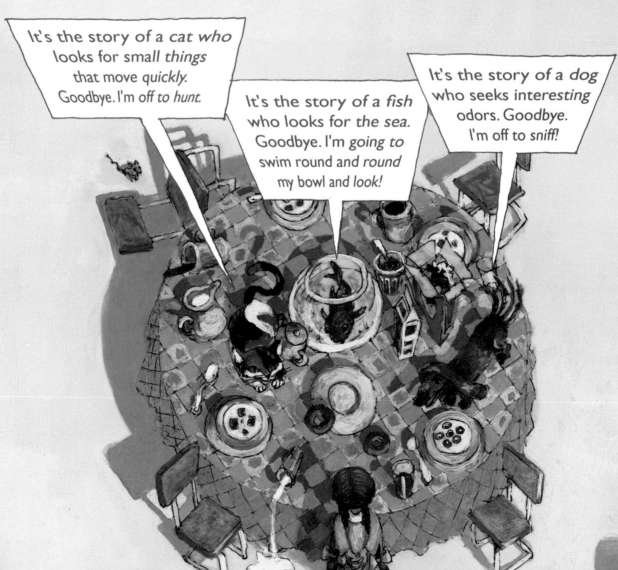

And off went
the girl
to the
next page.

There she met a large goose.

They rushed to the next page.

There the goose laid an egg.

The girl ran
to the next page.

The girl hurried on.

On the next page, a large white rabbit
grabbed the girl's hand and pulled
her toward a deep rabbit hole.

Just in time, the girl broke away, and
the rabbit went down the hole . . .

. . . and on the girl ran to the next page.

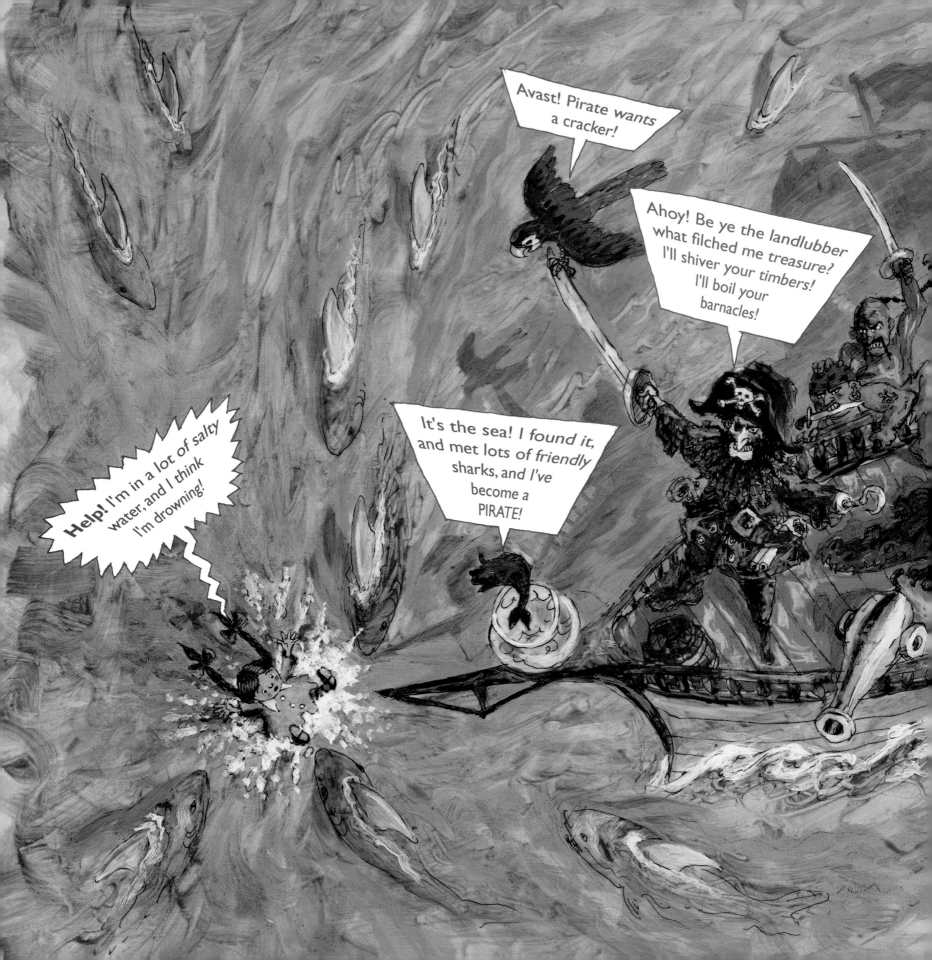

On the next page
she found her brother.

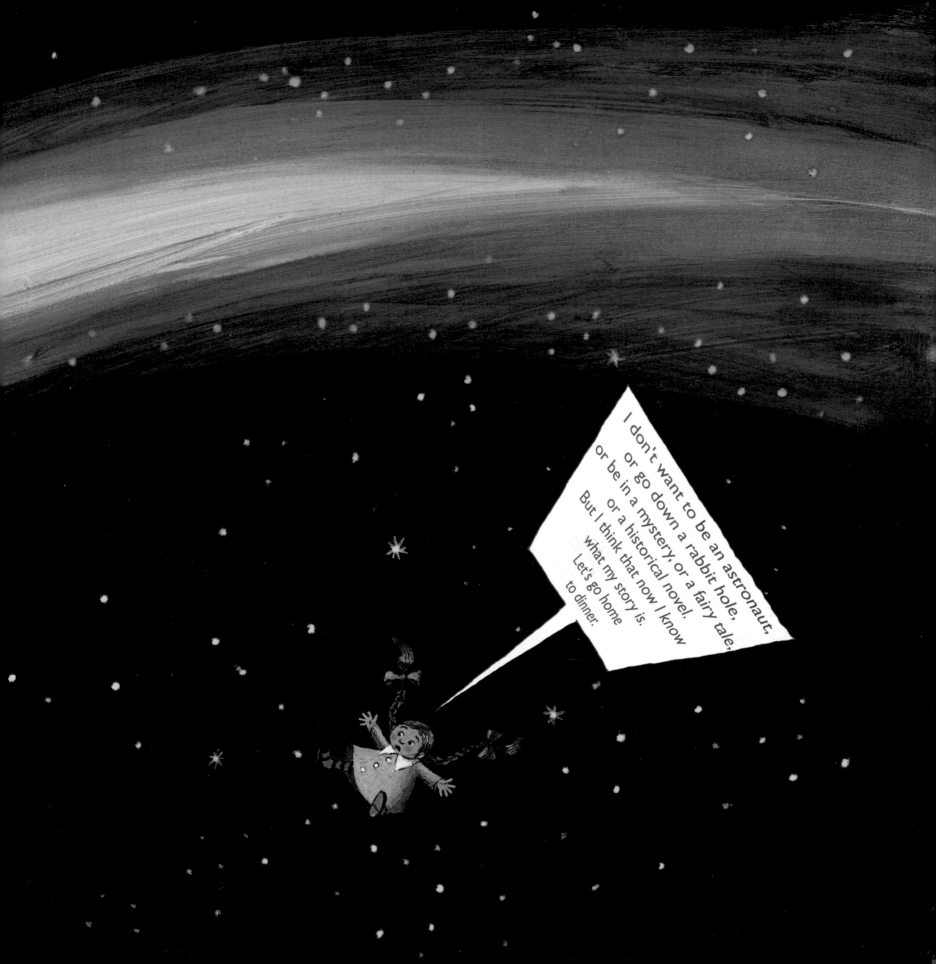

At dinner, the girl made an announcement.

And right after dinner, while the rest
of the family watched TV . . .

. . . the girl lay down on the rug,
opened her notebook, and began
to write.

On and on she wrote . . .

. . . until it was time for bed.

With loving gratitude to
Donald Graham and Richards Ruben
from whom I learned everything
about drawing
that can be taught.

Copyright © 2009 by Mordicai Gerstein
Published by Roaring Brook Press
Roaring Brook Press is a division of Holtzbrinck Publishing Holdings
Limited Partnership
175 Fifth Avenue, New York, New York 10010

Distributed in Canada by H. B. Fenn and Company Ltd.

Cataloging-in-Publication Data is on file at the Library of Congress
ISBN-10: 1-59643-251-9
ISBN-13: 978-1-59643-251-2

Roaring Brook Press books are available for special promotions and premiums.
For details contact: Director of Special Markets, Holtzbrinck Publishers.

First Edition April 2009
Book design by John Grandits
Printed in China
10 9 8 7 6 5 4 3 2 1